Chapter 1:

It began on a dreary October evening, with rain lashing against my apartment windows and the oppressive gloom of the city pressing in on all sides. The relentless urban sprawl of Arkham, with its decaying Victorian architecture and labyrinthine streets, was a place I had come to both love and loathe in equal measure. As a professor of anthropology at Miskatonic University, my life was steeped in the study of ancient cultures and civilisations, yet I had always prided myself on my rationality and scepticism. The occult and the supernatural were subjects of academic curiosity, nothing more. Little did I know that this conviction was about to be shattered.

The artefact arrived in a plain, unmarked box, with no return address and only my name scrawled in an unfamiliar, spidery hand. It was a curious thing, given that I had not been expecting any packages. As I held the box, an inexplicable sense of foreboding washed over me. Perhaps it was the weight of the package, too heavy for its size, or the almost palpable aura of unease it exuded. Regardless, I carried it into my study, eager to uncover its contents.

The box contained a small, intricately carved idol, unlike anything I had ever seen. It was made of a strange, greenish-black stone that seemed to absorb the light around it, giving it an almost otherworldly appearance. The figure was vaguely humanoid, but its proportions were grotesque, with elongated limbs and a face that defied description—its features a disturbing amalgamation of human and something far more alien.

Along with the idol was a letter, written in an archaic script that I could barely decipher. The paper was old and brittle, the ink faded, yet the message was clear and urgent. It spoke of an ancient cult that worshipped the idol, of forbidden knowledge that could drive a man to madness. The writer implored me to destroy the artefact, warning that it was a gateway to horrors beyond human comprehension. Despite the ominous tone of the letter, my curiosity was piqued. The idea of uncovering a mystery that had eluded others was too tempting to resist. I decided to study the idol further, not realising that this decision would set me on a path of unspeakable terror.

Over the next few days, I immersed myself in research, consulting every book and manuscript I could find on ancient religions and obscure artefacts. I spent countless hours in the university's musty library, pouring over tomes that chronicled the myths and legends of forgotten civilisations. The more I learned, the more obsessed I became. The idol seemed to have a power over me, compelling me to uncover its secrets. Yet, a part of me was reluctant to delve too deeply. The warnings in the letter echoed in my mind, and I began to experience strange, unsettling dreams.

In these dreams, I found myself in a vast, alien landscape, surrounded by towering monoliths and shadowy figures. The air was thick with a palpable sense of dread, and I felt an overwhelming urge to flee, yet my legs refused to move. Each night, the dreams grew more vivid and terrifying, and I awoke drenched in sweat, my heart pounding in my chest. I tried to convince myself that it was merely the result of my overactive imagination, but the fear gnawed at me.

The more I studied the idol, the more I felt its influence creeping into my thoughts and dreams. It was as if the artefact had a life of its own, a malignant consciousness that sought to ensnare me. I became withdrawn, neglecting my duties at the university and isolating myself from friends and colleagues. My once orderly life began to unravel, consumed by the dark allure of the idol.

One particularly stormy night, as I sat hunched over my desk, surrounded by ancient texts, and scribbled notes, a sudden knock at the door startled me. My heart raced as I hesitated, the sense of foreboding growing stronger. Taking a deep breath, I opened the door, half expecting to find some shadowy figure from my nightmares standing there.

Instead, it was an elderly man, his long white beard and piercing blue eyes lending him an almost otherworldly presence. He introduced himself as Dr Nathaniel Armitage, a retired professor of occult studies. He had heard about the artefact through an old colleague and had come to offer his assistance. His knowledge of the occult and his calm, authoritative demeanour provided a welcome respite from the growing madness that surrounded me.

Chapter 2:

Despite Dr Armitage's assurances, a part of me remained reluctant to delve deeper into the mysteries of the idol. The rational part of my mind, the part that had been honed through years of academic training and scientific inquiry, resisted the notion that this artefact could be anything more than an interesting historical curiosity. Yet, the inexplicable dreams and the unsettling aura of the idol continued to haunt me, eroding my confidence in the safety of continuing my research.

Dr Armitage seemed to sense my hesitation. Over the course of several days, he shared his extensive knowledge of the occult and the supernatural, recounting tales of ancient civilisations and forbidden rites that defied explanation. He spoke of the Cult of the Shattered Veil, an ancient and secretive group that worshipped beings from beyond our reality. According to him, the idol was not merely a relic but a conduit to these otherworldly entities, capable of bridging the gap between our world and theirs.

As fascinating as his stories were, they only served to deepen my unease. The rational part of me clung desperately to the belief that there was a logical explanation for everything I had experienced. I considered abandoning my research entirely, destroying the idol as the letter had implored me to do, and returning to my normal, orderly life. But the obsession had already taken root, and the pull of the unknown was too strong to resist.

In a final attempt to convince me, Dr Armitage arranged for a series of meetings with individuals who had encountered similar artefacts and survived to tell the tale. These people, a disparate group of scholars, adventurers, and occultists, had all been touched by the darkness in some way. Their stories were harrowing, filled with accounts of madness, death, and the inexplicable. Yet, they had also gained a profound understanding of the true nature of reality and the fragile barrier that separated our world from the horrors that lurked beyond.

Despite their warnings and the palpable fear in their eyes, my curiosity was only heightened. The notion that there were secrets beyond the grasp of science and reason, truths that defied the natural order, was both terrifying and exhilarating. I found myself drawn deeper into the web of mystery and danger, unable to turn back.

Chapter 3:

Dr Armitage became my guide and mentor in this strange new world. His knowledge of the occult and his calm, authoritative demeanour provided a welcome anchor in the storm of madness that surrounded me. Together, we began a systematic study of the idol, conducting a series of rituals and experiments to unlock its secrets.

We scoured the university's extensive collection of rare books and manuscripts, delving into the arcane and the forbidden. Dr Armitage introduced me to texts I had never before considered, tomes that chronicled the hidden history of the world and the dark forces that sought to control it. He taught me the languages of the ancients and the symbols of power that could bind or banish the entities from beyond.

As we delved deeper into the mysteries of the artefact, strange phenomena began to occur. Objects moved on their own, whispers echoed in the darkness, and shadows seemed to writhe with a life of their own. The air grew heavy with a palpable sense of dread, and the boundaries of reality seemed to blur. Yet, through it all, Dr Armitage remained steadfast, his unwavering belief in the importance of our work providing a beacon of hope.

One evening, as we performed a particularly complex ritual, the air in the room grew cold, and an unnatural silence descended. The idol began to glow with an eerie, greenish light, and I felt a presence watching us. Dr Armitage chanted in a language I did not recognize, his voice steady and authoritative. The very fabric of reality seemed to ripple and tear, and I caught a glimpse of the dark, chaotic void beyond.

At that moment, I crossed the threshold from the mundane world of science and reason into a realm of unspeakable horror. The veil between our world and another had been shattered, and I saw shapes and forms that defied comprehension, beings of such immense power and malevolence that my mind struggled to grasp their existence. The experience left me shaken to my core, yet also strangely exhilarated. I had seen beyond the veil and glimpsed the true nature of reality, and there was no turning back.

Chapter 4:

The night of the ritual marked a turning point in our journey. With the boundaries between our world and another shattered, we were plunged into a realm of unspeakable horror and wonder. The presence we had felt during the ritual lingered, a constant reminder of the dark forces we had unleashed. The idol, once a mere curiosity, now seemed to pulse with malevolent energy, a beacon drawing us deeper into the abyss.

Our studies took on a new urgency. We realised that we were not merely seeking knowledge for its own sake but were engaged in a battle for the very survival of our world. The cult mentioned in the letter, the Cult of the Shattered Veil, was real, and they were aware of our activities. We began to receive threats—anonymous letters filled with cryptic warnings, shadowy figures watching us from a distance, and strange occurrences that defied explanation. It became clear that the cult would stop at nothing to reclaim the idol and use its power to summon their dark gods.

Dr Armitage and I were forced to go into hiding, moving from one safe house to another as we continued our research. We relied on the network of allies we had cultivated—other scholars, adventurers, and occultists who shared our mission to protect humanity from the forces of darkness. These individuals provided us with shelter, resources, and valuable information about the cult and their activities.

Our quest led us to ancient libraries, forgotten tombs, and hidden temples, each filled with their own dangers and secrets. We encountered traps and guardians, both human and supernatural, designed to protect the knowledge we sought. Yet, through it all, Dr Armitage's unwavering resolve and deep understanding of the occult guided us. His mentorship was invaluable, and I came to rely on his wisdom and experience.

The journey was not without its toll. The constant danger and the knowledge of the horrors that lurked just beyond the veil weighed heavily on us. We were haunted by the memories of what we had seen and the knowledge of the dark forces that sought to destroy us. Yet, despite the fear and the uncertainty, we pressed on, driven by a sense of duty and the hope that we could avert the impending catastrophe.

Chapter 5:

As we delved deeper into the mysteries of the idol and the Cult of the Shattered Veil, we faced a series of tests that challenged our resolve and our sanity. The cultists were relentless in their pursuit, using both mundane and supernatural means to thwart our progress. We were forced to remain constantly vigilant, always one step ahead of their agents.

Our journey took us to the remote corners of the world, from the frozen wastes of Antarctica to the dense jungles of South America. In each place, we sought out ancient relics and forbidden knowledge that could aid us in our quest. We encountered other artefacts similar to the idol, each with its own unique properties and dangers. These items provided us with valuable clues about the nature of the Great Old Ones and the cult's plans.

Along the way, we met others who had been touched by the darkness. Some were allies, willing to share their knowledge and aid us in our fight. These individuals came from all walks of life—scholars, adventurers, occultists, and even former cultists who had renounced their allegiance. Each had their own reasons for joining our cause, whether it was a desire for redemption, a thirst for knowledge, or a simple sense of duty. Together, we formed a loose but determined network, united by our common goal.

Others we encountered were enemies, twisted and corrupted by their association with the cult. These individuals were often powerful and dangerous, wielding dark magic and forbidden knowledge. They sought to stop us at every turn, using deception, violence, and supernatural forces to achieve their aims. The battles we fought were fierce and desperate, testing our strength and resolve.

Through these trials, I learned the true extent of the cult's power and the depths of their depravity. They worshipped beings known as the Great Old Ones, ancient and malevolent entities that sought to reclaim our world. The idol was a conduit, a key to unlocking the barriers between dimensions and allowing these beings to enter our reality. The cult's ultimate goal was to summon these dark gods and bring about an age of chaos and destruction.

Despite the constant danger, we made progress in our quest. We uncovered ancient texts that provided insight into the rituals and symbols used by the cult. We discovered hidden sanctuaries filled with relics and artefacts that could aid us in our fight. Each victory, no matter how small, brought us closer to understanding the true nature of the threat we faced and how to stop it.

Chapter 6:

Our quest ultimately led us to an ancient, abandoned temple hidden deep in the forests of New England. According to our research, this temple was the heart of the cult's power and the location of a powerful artefact that could either save or doom humanity. It was here that the final confrontation would take place, and the fate of our world would be decided.

The journey to the temple was fraught with peril. The forest itself seemed to conspire against us, the trees closing in and the underbrush tangling our path. We navigated treacherous terrain, evaded cultists, and faced creatures that defied explanation. Each step brought us closer to the heart of darkness, the air growing thicker with a palpable sense of evil. It was as if the land itself was corrupted by the dark power that emanated from the temple.

As we neared our destination, the sense of dread grew stronger. The forest became eerily silent, the usual sounds of wildlife replaced by an oppressive, unnatural stillness. The very ground seemed to writhe beneath our feet as if the earth itself was alive and aware of our presence. It was a place where the boundaries between our world and another had been worn thin, where the veil had been shattered, and the darkness seeped through.

We finally arrived at the temple, a massive structure of ancient stone, covered in moss and vines. The entrance was guarded by grotesque statues, their features twisted and malevolent. Inside, the air was thick with the stench of decay and the echoes of unspeakable horrors. The walls were lined with carvings that depicted scenes of ritual sacrifice and dark rites, the symbols and runes glowing faintly with an otherworldly light.

At the centre of the temple was a vast, cavernous chamber, filled with the remnants of ancient rituals and dark rites. The air was heavy with a palpable sense of dread, and the very ground seemed to pulse with a malevolent energy. At the centre of the chamber stood a massive, stone altar, upon which rested the artefact—a crystalline shard that pulsed with an unearthly light. It was the key to the cult's power and the source of the dark forces that threatened our world.

Chapter 7:

The final confrontation took place within the dark, foreboding confines of the temple's central chamber. As we approached the stone altar, the air grew cold, and an unnatural silence descended upon us. The artefact, a crystalline shard that pulsed with an eerie, unearthly light, was the focal point of the room, and I could feel its malevolent energy reaching out to us.

Suddenly, the shadows that filled the chamber began to shift and coalesce, forming into monstrous shapes. These were the guardians of the artefact, servants of the Great Old Ones, and they were determined to stop us. The sight of these creatures, with their twisted forms and glowing eyes, filled me with a primal terror. Yet, there was no turning back.

Dr Armitage and I fought with all our might, using every ounce of knowledge and power we had acquired. The battle was fierce and desperate, the guardians' otherworldly strength and speed testing us to our limits. Dr Armitage chanted incantations in a language I did not understand, his voice steady and authoritative, while I wielded the symbols and rituals he had taught me. The very air seemed to crackle with energy as our spells clashed with the dark forces that filled the chamber.

In the midst of the chaos, I managed to reach the altar and grasp the shard. As I did, a searing pain shot through my body, and I felt my mind teetering on the brink of madness. The shard pulsed with an unholy light, and I could feel the presence of the Great Old Ones pressing down on me, their malevolent will threatening to consume me. My vision blurred, and I struggled to maintain my grip on reality.

With a final, desperate effort, I managed to harness the power of the shard and sever the connection between our world and the realm of the Great Old Ones. The temple shook with the force of the rupture, and the guardians dissolved into shadow. The oppressive weight that had hung over us lifted, and a sense of peace and clarity washed over me. The battle was over, and we had emerged victorious, but the cost had been high.

Chapter 8:

In the aftermath of the battle, Dr Armitage and I stood amidst the ruins of the temple, battered and exhausted but triumphant. We had succeeded in our quest, and the immediate threat had been averted. The artefact, now devoid of its malevolent energy, was safely hidden away, where it could no longer be used to bring about the end of our world.

As we made our way back through the forest, the oppressive sense of dread that had haunted us began to dissipate. The air grew warmer, and the natural sounds of the forest returned, a welcome reminder that we had restored balance to our world. Despite the physical and mental toll of our journey, a sense of accomplishment filled me. We had faced the darkness and emerged victorious, armed with knowledge and a renewed sense of purpose.

Upon returning to civilisation, we were met with a mixture of disbelief and awe. Our colleagues at Miskatonic University were sceptical of our accounts, but the undeniable evidence of our experiences—the artefact, the texts, and the scars we bore—lent credibility to our story. We began the arduous task of documenting our findings, compiling a comprehensive record of the cult, the Great Old Ones, and the rituals we had encountered.

Dr Armitage and I became close friends, bound by the shared trauma of our ordeal and the knowledge that we had saved the world from an unimaginable fate. Our bond was forged in the crucible of darkness, and we knew that our work was far from over. The immediate threat may have been averted, but the cult still existed, and the forces of darkness remained ever-vigilant, seeking new ways to breach the veil.

Chapter 9:

The journey back to normalcy was a slow and arduous process. The knowledge we had gained came with a heavy burden, and the memories of what we had faced haunted us. Nightmares plagued my sleep, and the shadows of the past loomed large in my mind. Yet, there was also a sense of hope and determination. We had faced the darkness and emerged stronger, and we were determined to use our knowledge to protect the world from future threats.

Dr Armitage and I continued our research, delving deeper into the mysteries of the occult and the supernatural. We established a network of allies, individuals who had encountered the darkness and survived, and together we formed a loose but determined organization dedicated to combating the forces of evil. We called ourselves the Guardians of the Veil, and our mission was to protect humanity from the horrors that lurked beyond our reality.

Our efforts were not without challenges. The cult remained a constant threat, their agents ever watchful and determined to reclaim the artefact and continue their dark rituals. We faced numerous battles, both physical and psychological, as we sought to thwart their plans and protect the fragile barrier between our world and the abyss.

Despite the dangers, we pressed on, driven by a sense of duty and the knowledge that we were the last line of defence against the encroaching darkness. Our work took us to the far corners of the globe, uncovering ancient relics and forbidden knowledge that could aid us in our fight. Each victory, no matter how small, was a step towards securing the safety of our world.

Chapter 10:

The true test of our resolve came when we discovered that the cult had managed to obtain another artefact, one even more powerful than the idol we had encountered. This artefact, an ancient tome known as the Necronomicon, contained knowledge that could potentially summon the Great Old Ones and bring about the end of our world.

The battle to obtain the Necronomicon was fierce and desperate. The cult had grown stronger and more organized, their agents more ruthless and determined. We faced numerous challenges, both physical and supernatural, as we sought to prevent the artefact from falling into their hands. The fight took us to the very edge of sanity, as we confronted horrors that defied comprehension.

In the end, we emerged victorious, but the cost was high. Dr Armitage, my mentor and friend, sacrificed himself to ensure that the Necronomicon was destroyed. His loss was a devastating blow, but his sacrifice was not in vain. With the destruction of the Necronomicon, we dealt a significant blow to the cult and prevented a catastrophe of unimaginable proportions.

Chapter 11:

In the aftermath of our final battle, I found myself reflecting on the journey we had undertaken. We had faced unspeakable horrors and emerged victorious, armed with knowledge and a renewed sense of purpose. The world would never be the same, but we had learned to live with the knowledge that there were forces beyond our comprehension, forces that we must remain vigilant against.

As I sit here, penning this account of our journey, I am reminded of the old adage: "Knowledge is power." But with that power comes great responsibility, and a burden that we must carry for the rest of our lives. The veil between worlds may have been shattered, but it is our duty to ensure that it remains intact, protecting humanity from the horrors that lie beyond.

The Guardians of the Veil continue to watch over the world, ever vigilant against the encroaching darkness. Our journey has shown us that the battle against evil is never truly over, and there will always be those who seek to bring about the end of our world. But as long as we stand united, armed with knowledge and the courage to face the unknown, there is hope.

And so, the story continues, with new heroes rising to face the darkness, armed with the knowledge that we have passed down. For as long as the Guardians of the Veil exist, there will always be those who stand against the forces of darkness, guarding the fragile barrier between our world and the abyss.

THE END

Printed in Great Britain
by Amazon